THE SINGING SHEPHERD

ANGELA ELWELL HUNT

The Singing Shepherd

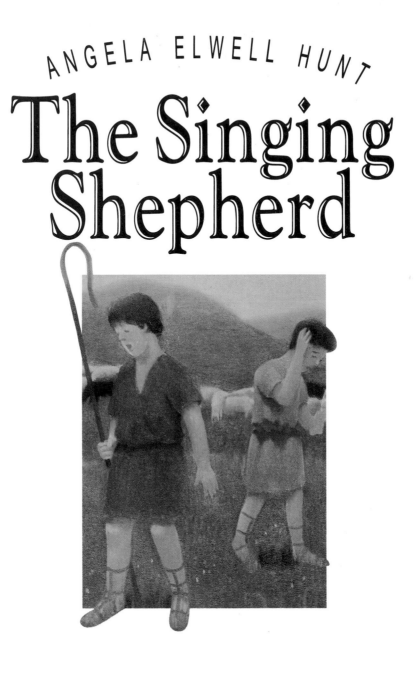

ILLUSTRATIONS BY

Peter Palagonia

A LION PICTURE STORY

FOR HIM
whose perfect love casts out fear

———————

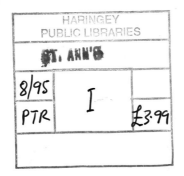

Whenever he was afraid, Jareb sang. Singing made him feel better.

But his singing made everyone else feel worse. Jareb's singing was dreadful.

Jareb was a shepherd. He helped his older brothers Ariel, Samuel and Simon tend their father's sheep on the hillsides of Bethlehem. Jareb loved the calm, quiet sheep.

But a shepherd's life can be frightening at times. Nights were filled with dark shadows and eerie noises. The rumble of thunder, the howls of jackals, and the hooting of owls caused Jareb to sing a lot.

Ariel and Samuel hated Jareb's squeaky songs. "But the sheep like them," Simon pointed out. "They know no wild animal would come near us while Jareb is yowling. Let him sing."

So Jareb sang day and night. He even hummed in his sleep. His brothers stuffed wool in their ears.

One cool night the shepherds settled their flock and lay down to rest by the campfire. Ariel, Samuel and Simon fell asleep. Jareb hummed off-key as his eyes grew heavy. The velvet darkness of night wrapped around him, and Jareb yawned.

Before he could close his mouth, the sky flashed brighter than a thousand campfires, and an angel stood right in front of Jareb. His clothes glowed with a blinding blue flame. He shone like the sun.

Jareb was terrified. He tried to sing, but his mouth wouldn't move. He heard his brothers gasp.

"Do not be afraid," the visitor said. "I bring you good news of great joy for all people. This night a Saviour has been born in Bethlehem. He is Christ the Lord."

"Wh-wh-what?" Ariel asked. "A Saviour?"

The shining man looked at Ariel and smiled. "Here is a sign to help you find him. The baby will be wrapped in cloths and lying in a manger."

Immediately the whole sky blazed with light, and hundreds of angels like the dazzling visitor filled the pasture and the hills. They were everywhere, in radiant white, and they seemed to look right at Jareb.

"Glory to God in the highest!" their voices rang through the still night, "and on earth, peace to all people everywhere."

The brilliant visitors shone brighter and brighter until they seemed to melt into a burning sky. Jareb and his brothers shielded their eyes. Then, in an instant, all was as dark as before.

"This is wonderful!" Ariel shouted, jumping to his feet. "The Saviour has come. Let's go and find him!"

"How many babies in a manger can there be?" Samuel said, brushing grass from his clothes.

"The prophets said he'd come to Bethlehem," Simon added, reaching for his sandals. "Can you believe an angel came to *us*?"

Jareb didn't move. He began to sing softly.

"Come on, Jareb," Samuel urged. "Are you afraid? Too afraid to find this Saviour?"

"No," Jareb answered. "I'd rather stay here with the sheep, that's all."

Ariel, Samuel and Simon turned and hurried to Bethlehem, their hearts full of excitement. Jareb stayed with the sheep, singing in the dark.

Jareb's brothers couldn't stop talking when they returned. "You should have seen him," Ariel told Jareb.

"You should not be such a coward, Jareb," Simon added. "*You* were invited to see the Saviour, too. If God can send angels to invite you, can't he also give you a little courage?"

Jareb thought about the baby for many months. The more he thought, the more ashamed he felt. Why was he always afraid? Why did he spend all his time singing to silly sheep?

Jareb didn't want to be afraid any longer. One evening after the sheep were settled, he put on his cloak.

"Where are you going?" asked Samuel. "It will be dark soon."

"I am going to find that baby," Jareb answered. And off he went to Bethlehem, singing off-key.

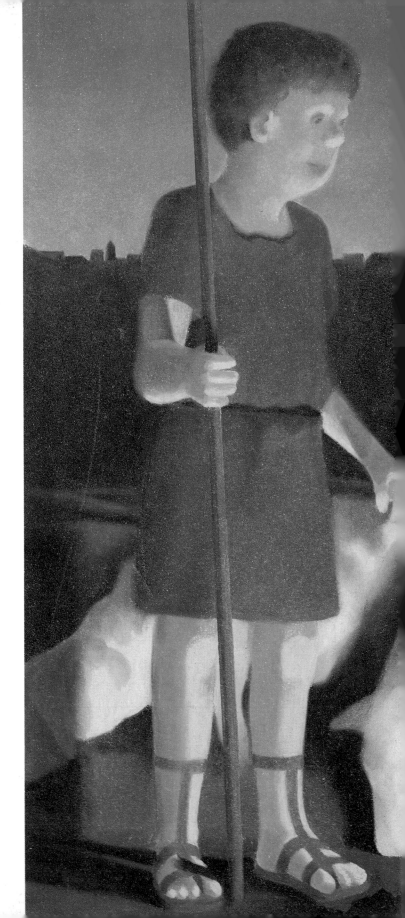

Jareb had no idea how to find a child who had been born so many months before. He didn't even know if the family still lived in Bethlehem. He prayed that God would guide his footsteps.

The road into Bethlehem was crowded. A rich caravan of men and camels was coming out of the town, and Jareb had to stop and wait for it to pass. Suddenly a young camel slipped away from the others and bolted straight at Jareb.

"Quick! Stop that camel!"

Without thinking, Jareb caught the rope dangling from the camel's neck.

"Thank you, young man," the servant said, taking the camel from Jareb. "My masters are rich men, but they would be angry if I lost their prized camel. Although," the servant scratched his head, "since we left the child's house, my masters have not stopped smiling."

"Oh?" Jareb asked, hardly daring to hope. "What child is that?"

"A wonderful, beautiful child." The servant smiled at Jareb. "He will be a great king some day, my masters say. We have come a great distance to find him."

Jareb's heart beat faster as the servant told him where to find the child. Could this be the Saviour?

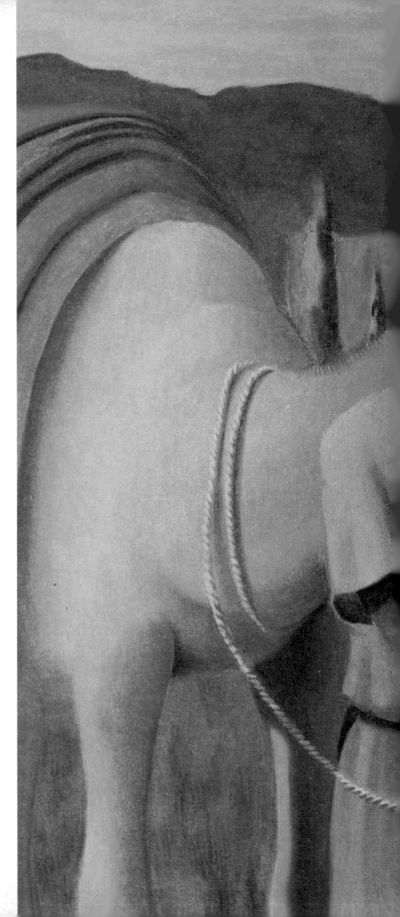

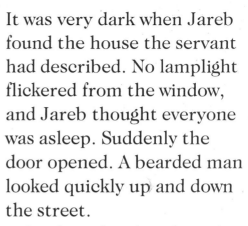

It was very dark when Jareb found the house the servant had described. No lamplight flickered from the window, and Jareb thought everyone was asleep. Suddenly the door opened. A bearded man looked quickly up and down the street.

Jareb took a deep breath and stepped forward. "Please, sir," he said, "may I see the child?"

The bearded man frowned. "Who sent you?" he asked.

Jareb felt his cheeks burning with shame. "An angel. Many months ago. But I was afraid to come."

The man pulled Jareb inside.

"I am Joseph," he said. "Here is my wife Mary. And this is Jesus."

In the starlight streaming through the window, Jareb saw a young woman holding a sleeping child. The woman smiled shyly at Jareb.

Joseph spoke again. "An angel has warned me that King Herod will send soldiers to kill all baby boys in Bethlehem. Mary and I must take Jesus away from here. But there may be soldiers at the city gate already. You must help us."

"Soldiers?" Jareb felt his knees begin to quiver. "Killing? King Herod?" Jareb's words trailed off, and he began to hum nervously.

"We must leave tonight," Joseph interrupted. "God has sent you to us. Will you help?"

Jareb thought for a moment. Then he pulled a rough shawl from his shoulder. "This is a sling for newborn lambs," he explained. "With it I could carry Jesus outside the city. No one would expect me to be carrying a baby."

Joseph smiled. "Your plan is good, my young friend," he said. Joseph and Mary carefully placed Jesus in the sling.

"There is a well outside the city gate," Jareb whispered. "I will meet you there."

Mary and Joseph slipped out into the darkness. Jareb carefully shifted the sling onto his shoulder and peered down the street. He could hear noise far away— screaming and the clash of swords. Jareb was more frightened than he had ever been in his life. He prayed the baby wouldn't cry. Then he set out for the city gate, humming softly as he walked.

At the gate, a rough guard stepped in front of Jareb and squinted down at him. "We are looking for babies," he growled, "baby boys. What's that you're carrying?"

"Please, sir," Jareb stammered. "I'm . . . I'm just a shepherd. And this is a sling for carrying lambs."

Jareb felt his fingers begin to tremble. He squeezed the strap of the sling and tried to smile. "I'm famous for my sheep songs. Just listen."

Jareb burst into song. Fear made his voice louder and scratchier and even more out of tune than usual. The guard shuddered in disgust and covered his ears. "Arrgh!" he shouted. "Away with you, crazy shepherd. Stop that awful racket!"

Outside the city, Joseph and Mary were waiting anxiously by the well. Jareb gently lifted Jesus from the sling.

"Here's your little lamb," he said, placing the child in Mary's arms. Jareb laughed. "Look how he smiles at the world's worst singer!"

"You are a very brave young man." Mary smiled and her eyes filled with tears. "And your voice is a blessing from God."

Jareb watched until the small family disappeared on the road, then he turned to the fields where his sheep waited.

Jareb's ears rang with Mary's words, "You are a brave young man. And your voice is a blessing from God."

The night was filled with dark shadows. Calls of owls and jackals echoed through the hills. But Jareb didn't notice. He began to sing—not because he was afraid, but because he was happy. He had been brave. He had helped the Saviour.

As Jareb walked, his singing grew louder and stronger. The fearsome noises of the night vanished as owls and jackals fled to distant hills. The only sound the waiting sheep heard that night was Jareb's happy song.

Text copyright © 1992 Angela Elwell Hunt
Illustrations copyright © 1992 Peter Palagonia

Published by
Lion Publishing plc
Sandy Lane West, Oxford, England
ISBN 0 7459 3036 0
Albatross Books Pty Ltd
PO Box 320, Sutherland, NSW 2232, Australia
ISBN 0 7324 0850 4

First edition 1992
First paperback edition 1994

All rights reserved

A catalogue record for this book is available
from the British Library

Printed and bound in Malaysia